OTHER BOOKS IN

Disney's Aladdin

SERIES

Disney's

Aladdin

JASMINE AND THE
DISAPPEARING TIGER

by Leslie McGuire

Illustrations by
Brooks Campbell and Kenny Thompkins

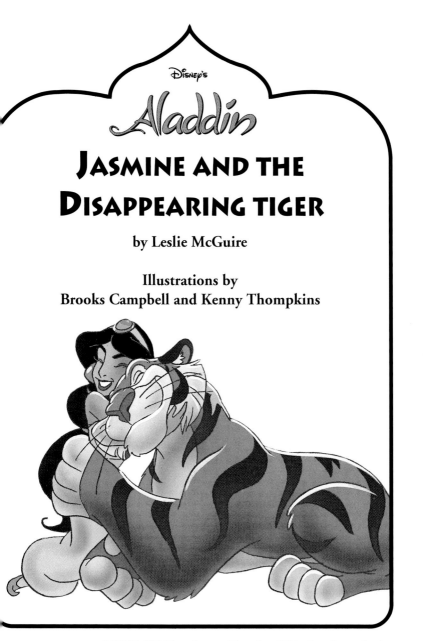

©1993 The Walt Disney Company. No portion of this book may be reproduced
without written consent of The Walt Disney Company. Produced by Mega-Books
of New York, Inc. Design and Art Direction by Michaelis/Carpelis Design Assoc.,
Inc. Printed in the United States of America.

ISBN 1-56326-252-5

CHAPTER 1

rying pans from Persia!"

"Coffee beans from deepest Mocha!"

"Step right up and get your two-for-one special at Abdul-in-the-Box!" screeched a voice in Aladdin's ear. "Falafel, lettuce, cheese, and Special Sauce on a poppy-seed pita!"

"Ooh, let's stop and get one," said Princess Jasmine.

"I'm not hungry," Aladdin answered. He pulled Jasmine into a narrow alley. "Besides, Abdul hates me."

Aladdin and Jasmine were strolling

through the colorful marketplace of Agrabah. Aladdin had once been a beggar in these streets. That was before he found the magic lamp and the Genie. Now that Aladdin was a prince, most of the shopkeepers liked him a lot better and were only too happy to show him their wares.

"What a stick in the mud," said Jasmine, stopping to admire a silk scarf. "So what am I supposed to eat?"

"Don't worry," said Aladdin, laughing. "There are plenty of good things to eat here. Follow me!"

Off they ran. Aladdin's pet monkey, Abu, scampered along behind them. One outraged yell after another came from the stalls as Abu snatched a piece of fruit, a loaf of bread, or a pastry. It was just for old-time's sake. Abu had more than enough to eat at the palace, and Aladdin always saw that the merchants were paid.

Aladdin, Jasmine, and Abu dodged in and out of alleys, behind stalls, and through doorways.

Jasmine saw a crowd forming in front of them and stopped suddenly.

"Wait a minute, Aladdin," she said. "What's going on over there? Look, it's a magician!"

"I thought you were hungry," said Aladdin. "I know this great little place — "

"Maybe later," said Jasmine. "Do you see what he's doing? He's making that basket leap in the air!"

A short young man dressed in rags was at the end of the alley. His eyes were closed, his hands were stretched out, and his long fingers were wiggling as the basket at his feet hopped up and down.

"It looks like it's alive!" Jasmine gasped.

"That's the oldest trick on the planet," said Aladdin. He yawned. "He's probably got a frog in there."

The magician pulled a silk scarf out of his sleeve and waved it in the air. A dozen bright green birds fluttered out. They soared into the air and disappeared over the towers of the mosque.

Jasmine ran up to the magician. "Please, do another trick."

"Your wish is...my command," mumbled the magician. He rolled his eyes, held his fingers in the air, and waited.

"I can't believe it," Aladdin groaned. "You think this guy is good? I've seen better magic tricks at the bakery!"

"Why the bakery?" asked Jasmine. "Bakers don't do magic."

"Neither does this guy!" said Aladdin.

"Shhh," said Jasmine. "He's about to do something wonderful!"

A tree blossomed from the magician's outstretched fingers on one hand. Pears, oranges, and pomegranates hung from the branches.

"Wow!" said a little boy. The crowd looked on, mouths open, in silence.

"Which is your favorite fruit?" the magician asked Jasmine. He had a lopsided smile.

"Pears!" cried Jasmine.

He reached up and plucked a pear. Bowing, he handed it to the amazed princess.

Jasmine bit into the pear. "That's the best

I've ever tasted."

Aladdin yawned again. "This guy is the dumbest magician I've ever seen," he muttered. "Can we leave now?"

"You're just jealous because he can do something you can't," said Jasmine. "I think he's great!"

"I am not jealous. I'm bored," snapped Aladdin.

Then the magician waved at a stall full of brass candlesticks and goblets. It disappeared!

"Hey!" yelled the brass merchant. "Bring them back!" The magician smiled. Then he pulled three rabbits out of his sleeve. And finally, he lay down, closed his eyes, and rose until he was suspended in midair.

Jasmine couldn't stop clapping. Aladdin couldn't stop frowning.

"Oh, any magician can do that," Aladdin muttered. "Can we go *now*?"

"Not yet," said Jasmine. "I think I'll invite him to the palace."

The magician was still lying in the air. Jasmine gave him a good yank on his shoe and he fell to the ground with a thud. His turban tipped over his face.

"What's happening?" the magician mumbled, still on the ground and trying to get his turban on straight.

"I'm Princess Jasmine," she said. "Please come to the palace this evening. My father would love your act."

"A princess? Well...er...I, uh..." The magician looked confused and scratched his head.

"Never mind," said Aladdin. He took Jasmine by the elbow and pulled. "The palace is booked for the next few weeks."

"The palace is definitely not booked!" Jasmine said. She jerked her arm free and turned to the magician. "Please say you'll be there at eight o'clock tonight."

"I...er...don't know if I'm...ready," said the magician, glancing around. "Not for the palace, anyway. I'm really not that good."

"You can say that again," said Aladdin.

"Don't listen to him!" snapped Jasmine. "Just do the same tricks you did for us here."

"Oh, boy!" said the magician. "What if I

mess up? Will I get in trouble?"

"Of course not!" said Jasmine.

"I hope so," mumbled Aladdin.

"Then it's a deal, right? See you at eight?" asked Jasmine.

"Er...I mean, okay, Your Majesty," stuttered the magician. He turned to leave.

"Hey! Where's my stall, you idiot?" screamed the brass merchant.

"Oh! Sorry!" said the magician sheepishly, snapping his fingers. "I forgot!"

As Jasmine, Aladdin, and Abu dashed down the alley, the brass stall reappeared.

CHAPTER 2

ight o'clock came and went at the Sultan's palace, but no one arrived. At eight-thirty, there was still no magician. Finally, at nine o'clock, there was a thumping at the palace gates.

A few moments later, a ragtag group wearing enormous turbans trailed into the throne room.

"Good evening, Princess," said the magician. "These are my back-up singers."

"Back-up singers?" said Aladdin.

"I...er...work better when there's music," said the magician. "I am Omar, and they are called the...er...Four Dates."

"What a great idea!" said Jasmine.

"How come they're called the Four Dates when there are only three of them?" asked Aladdin.

"The fourth Date quit," said Omar. "We still haven't found a replacement."

"I love good music," said the Sultan, rubbing his hands together. "And I really love a good magician!"

"Then, he's going to hate this guy," Aladdin muttered to Abu. "The Four Dates! What a dumb name!"

The three Dates who were left pulled out their instruments and began to play. The first had a flute that sounded like a sick cat. The second plucked an out-of-tune harp, and the third pounded on a drum with wooden spoons. The drum looked like a dented cooking pot.

Two of the Dates stopped playing. The drummer banged on the pot with his spoons. "Is that supposed to be a drum roll?" Aladdin asked the drummer.

Bowing his head, the drummer shouted over the banging. "And now for your entertainment and mystification...the great...the fabulous...the totally pungent Omar...and three out of the Four Dates!"

Abu jumped to a chandelier and began swinging.

"Go, Omar, go!" yelled the Sultan.

The Magic Carpet rolled itself up tightly in a corner. It hated loud noise.

Jasmine's pet tiger, Rajah, lay at her feet snarling quietly, paws over his ears.

"Let's get this over with," said Aladdin.

The singers moaned and yowled like camels in love.

The magician smiled weakly. "If I could have your...er...attention. Please?"

He raised his hands. *Poof.* A cloud of smoke appeared. When the smoke cleared, a purple elephant with pink spots stood in the middle of the room.

Abu chattered and began swinging faster.

The elephant wheezed. Then it puffed. It looked very confused, then its trunk began to quiver.

Uh-oh, thought Aladdin as the elephant

wheezed harder and harder. The smoke's bothering him! "Look out!" he yelled.

"AAAAAHHHH...CHOOOO!"

The smoke disappeared. So did the elephant. So did Abu. But the chandelier was still swinging wildly. A furious chattering came from behind the throne. It was Abu. His hair was standing on end.

"And for our next trick..." the drummer said, as he banged on the pot. "Omar will perform the impossible...the stunning...the totally ridiculous...Persian Rope Dance!"

The singers howled even louder. The floor heaved up. It bulged. Then it cracked. Four ropes emerged from the crack. They wound up to the ceiling, swaying in time to the music.

But instead of swaying together, they got all tangled up and flopped to the floor.

The ropes slowly slithered back into the crack. The music stopped.

"Haven't we seen enough tricks yet?" whispered Aladdin.

"Shhh!" hissed Jasmine.

"And now for my...er...best trick," announced Omar, "I will make this royal tiger disappear!"

Rajah quickly hid behind the throne.

"Now, don't be silly, Rajah," said Jasmine. She coaxed the tiger back to her side. "Sit still and join in!"

Not reassured, Rajah edged toward the window. Omar pointed his finger at him and said, "K-k-kapibble, k-k-kapabble, k-k-kaput!"

Rajah vanished.

"And now, I will...er...bring him back!" Omar said. His fingers were crossed. He clapped his hands.

The tiger reappeared, looking dazed.

"Whew!" one of the Dates said to another. "When he gets nervous — watch out! You never know what's going to happen."

The show was over. Everyone applauded. Omar and the Dates took fifteen curtain calls. The magician and his back-up group backed out of the throne room, and the great doors slammed shut behind them.

"Thank goodness that's over," said Aladdin.

"They were fabulous!" said Jasmine, her eyes shining. She did not look at her tiger, who was sitting in the corner shaking all over.

CHAPTER 3

hat simple-minded magician is a nitwit. His idea of a good magic trick is to bring a sneezing elephant into the throne room," Aladdin muttered. "Yeck!"

"Just think!" said Jasmine. "How many times have you seen four ropes dance out of a marble floor?"

"What a tangle that was...which reminds me," said Aladdin bending down to inspect the marble, "if there's a crack in this floor, I'll make that magician pay for it."

Jasmine breathed a bit more easily when Aladdin couldn't find any trace of a crack in the throne room floor.

"I'd better check the chandelier, too," said Aladdin. "Who knows what kind of damage he caused. At least the purple elephant didn't throw up."

The Magic Carpet unrolled and flew out of the corner. Aladdin hopped on, and they rose to the ceiling. He inspected every candle and chain.

"Is everything all right?" asked Jasmine.

"Seems to be fine," said Aladdin.

The Magic Carpet landed back on the floor. When Aladdin stepped off, he saw Rajah lying in the corner, trembling, paws over his face.

"Hey! What's wrong with Rajah?" asked Aladdin.

"Maybe disappearing made him seasick," said Jasmine. "Aladdin, will you ask someone to send for the royal veterinarian?"

Aladdin left the room to call a servant. In the meantime, Jasmine tried to soothe Rajah, but he shrank back and crawled under the throne.

"I knew there was something fishy about

that magician," said Aladdin when he returned. "I've never seen poor Rajah act this way."

Dr. Hakim, the royal veterinarian, ran into the throne room. He walked around the tiger slowly. Then he reached out and carefully touched him. Usually, Rajah tried to bite him. Rajah didn't like Dr. Hakim. He had once tried to make Rajah drink medicine that tasted bad.

When the tiger didn't try to pin him to the floor or chase him from the room, Dr. Hakim moved closer to him. The doctor checked Rajah's eyes, looked in his ears, opened his mouth — carefully — and looked at his tongue. Then Dr. Hakim said, "Excuse me, Your Highness. Please be so kind as to leave the room. I will need privacy."

"What could be wrong?" asked Jasmine as she paced the floor outside the throne room. "And what's taking so long?"

"I'm worried," said Aladdin.

The door opened. Dr. Hakim came out looking grave.

"I have good news and bad news," he said.

"What's wrong?" said Jasmine.

"Well," said Dr. Hakim. "I don't know how to tell you this. The good news is that the tiger is in good health."

"So what's the bad news?" asked Aladdin. He put his arm around Jasmine. "If that miserable excuse for a magician did anything —"

"It's hard to explain," said Dr. Hakim. "It's — well — you see, Rajah is now a girl!"

"WHAT?" said Aladdin and Jasmine together. "That's impossible."

"True, it's impossible," said Dr. Hakim. "But that's the fact of the matter."

Jasmine and Aladdin ran into the throne room. Rajah was definitely not himself. The strange tiger looked scared to death.

"It's true," cried Jasmine. "This is not my Rajah."

"Find that stupid magician," Aladdin shouted to the guards.

"Forget the guards," said Jasmine, throwing on her cloak. "If he's lost my Rajah, I'll feed him to the crocodiles!"

"We don't feed people to crocodiles anymore in this kingdom," said Aladdin. "We arrest them."

"Maybe we arrest other people," said Jasmine. "But *that* guy will be fed to the crocodiles if I don't get my Rajah back safely."

She ran out of the palace. Aladdin dashed after her.

"A grouchy princess is nothing to mess with," he muttered. "I'm not going to say I told you so!" he yelled at her.

CHAPTER 4

 ix feet from the door of the palace, Abu caught up with Aladdin and jumped on his shoulder.

"Are you worried about Rajah, too, little buddy?" said Aladdin. "Come on. We need all the help we can get."

Twelve feet from the palace gate, the Magic Carpet scooped them all up and carried them toward the marketplace.

"Where do you think we should look first?" asked Jasmine.

"We'll try the street of the brass merchants," said Aladdin. "That's where we first saw Omar. But after that, I have no idea."

The Magic Carpet flew down the street of

the brass merchants, but there was no trace of Omar. It coursed through every alley and down every street near the marketplace. It flew all around town. They asked everyone they saw, but there wasn't one person who had seen Omar and the Dates.

"We sure could use the Genie now," said Jasmine.

"The last I heard, he was in the Canary Islands," said Aladdin. "The postcard said he'd met a cutie who wore bananas on her hat. It may be weeks before we hear from him."

"A vacationing genie is not a helpful genie," Jasmine sighed.

"Don't worry," said Aladdin. "Everything will work out fine."

"How?" asked Jasmine. "We've looked all over Agrabah. After the town, there's only the desert."

"A piece of cake," said Aladdin.

"You mean a lot of sand," said Jasmine. "Still, with the Magic Carpet to fly us over the whole desert, I bet we'll find them before morning. All we need to do is find and follow their footprints."

"Footprints?" said Aladdin. "There must be thousands of footprints out there. And it's dark."

"True. But we're looking for four sets of human footprints," said Jasmine, "and maybe one set of tiger prints."

The Carpet circled the walls of Agrabah. By now, most of the city was fast asleep, and a full moon was rising. Finally, at the doors of the east gate, they saw four sets of footprints heading out into the desert.

But there were no tiger prints.

"Just because Rajah is gone doesn't mean he's with them," Aladdin pointed out. "It could mean he's lost. But we still have to find the magician to find Rajah."

"Do you think he can bring Rajah back?" asked Jasmine. "Why don't you just send for the Genie?

"I can handle this by myself," Aladdin said. "When we find that magician, I'll make him bring Rajah back."

The Magic Carpet sped over the dunes.

For about ten miles, the footprints were clear, but then they abruptly ended.

The Carpet circled the last footprints several times. It seemed Omar and the Dates had disappeared into thin air.

Just then, Jasmine noticed a palace to the east, looming above the distant dunes. "I think that should be our first stop," she said.

"Nice place," said Aladdin as the Carpet continued eastward.

The palace was surrounded by sharp, jagged rocks that jutted up from the sand like huge shards of glass.

The walls of the palace were steep and shiny black. It was carved out of sheer rock that rose hundreds of feet in the air.

The Carpet set them down in front of the black iron gate that faced the only road up the cliff.

"Is anybody home?" asked Aladdin, rattling the gate.

The gate slowly swung open. They stepped inside — and twenty muscle-bound guards surrounded them.

"These guys have muscles in their noses," said Aladdin. "Think they're friendly?"

A booming voice echoed through the hallway and out into the night. "Bring those miserable excuses for slime in and take them to the dungeon!"

"The Sheik!" said one of the guards.

"The Sheik of what?" asked Jasmine.

A tall man dressed in velvet robes stepped into the doorway and snarled, "You dared come to my palace after midnight. I'm trying to work. You will pay for your mistake — and I'll keep that pretty carpet for my collection, thank you!"

The Carpet fluttered in the Sheik's grasp. The guards grabbed Aladdin and Jasmine and shoved them through a door.

"Hey," yelled Aladdin. "Quit pushing."

"Oh, please! No!" cried Jasmine. "Let us go! How will we ever find Rajah?"

The guards shoved them down a dark stairway, with the Sheik's shrill laugh still ringing in their ears.

CHAPTER 5

 he guards hustled Aladdin, Jasmine, and Abu down endless flights of slippery stone steps.

Aladdin lightly punched the arm of the guard holding him.

"I bet that's not muscle at all," he said. "I bet it's nothing but baby fat."

The guard snarled and threw Aladdin through a doorway.

"It's very muscular baby fat," Aladdin said.

Jasmine was shoved in after him, and Abu came flying right behind her. The door slammed, then it opened again.

"Gimme back my turban, you little ape," snapped a guard. He grabbed Abu by the arm

and dangled him in the air. Abu dropped the turban. The guard scooped it up, and the door clanged shut. They were left in total darkness.

"I think we're in trouble," said Aladdin.

"I know we're in trouble," said Jasmine.

"When you're right, you're...er...right," came a voice out of the blackness.

"Who the heck are you?" asked Aladdin. "Your voice sounds familiar."

"It is I, Omar the Magician."

"Omar!" Jasmine exclaimed. "We've been looking for you!"

"Uh-oh," said Omar. "I just hate it when people are looking for me. Who's there?"

"It's Princess Jasmine, Omar."

"And Aladdin. What did you do with Rajah?" added Aladdin. "We know he wasn't traveling with you."

"What do you mean?" said Omar. "He was there when I left!"

"Wrong!" said Jasmine. "A tiger was there, but it wasn't Rajah."

"Are you sure?" Omar asked. "When

you've seen one tiger, you've seen them all."

"Rajah is a male tiger," said Jasmine. "The tiger you left in the palace is female."

"Oops," said Omar.

"You'd better bring him back!" snapped Jasmine. "Or I'll feed you to the crocodiles."

"Crocodiles?" Omar gulped.

"Crocodiles," Jasmine said. "Or how about this? You get us out of this dungeon using your magic, then bring Rajah back, and I'll forgive you for losing him in the first place."

"Good idea," said Aladdin.

"Great idea," said Omar. "Except for one small problem. If I could get you out of here, I would already have gotten myself out of here."

"Are you saying — and correct me if I'm wrong — that you're not a good enough magician to get any of us out of here?" asked Aladdin.

"That's about the speed of it," said Omar. "I used my magic to get the Four...er...Three Dates out of the dungeon. I thought they could find a way...well...to rescue me. But, you see, I've misplaced them somehow."

"We're sunk," said Aladdin. "Even if we could break down this door somehow and get up those stairs without getting caught by the guards, we'd still have to climb down those cliffs outside."

"The Magic Carpet!" said Jasmine. "We've got to get the Magic Carpet back!"

"Can't you whistle for it, or something?" asked Omar.

"No. And even if we could, I bet that Sheik has it locked up," said Aladdin.

For a while, the only sound they heard was the slow drip of water. It was not cheery.

Suddenly, light flickered through the barred window of the dungeon door.

"Anybody in there?" came a small, silvery voice. "Can I get you folks anything?"

Aladdin leapt to his feet and peered through the window. On the other side stood a pretty, smiling girl. Her cinnamon-colored hair fell to her shoulders. She wore a green cloak wrapped tightly around her. The light of the candle was reflected in her amber eyes.

"Can you get us anything?" Aladdin echoed. "You sure can. How about the keys to this place — and some pistachio pastry while you're at it."

"Who are you?" Jasmine asked.

"My name is Amber," said the girl. "I'm the Sheik's niece. I work in the accounting department. I'm learning the business."

"Can you bring us our carpet?" asked Jasmine. "It can fly us out of the palace."

"There are thousands of carpets in my uncle's collection. What does yours look like?" asked Amber.

"It's not too big," said Jasmine. "It's purple, with red flames and a gold edge. It has lamps in the center and a tiger head at each corner. It also has four gorgeous gold tassels — one on each corner."

"Oh, right," said Amber. "The new one we got tonight. My uncle wanted it appraised right away."

"Can you get it for us?" asked Aladdin.

"I'll get in trouble," said Amber. "But if you'll take me with you, I'll get it. You see, I really hate this place."

Aladdin looked at Jasmine.

She nodded. "It sounds as if Amber wants out of here as much as we do," she said. "Let's take a chance."

CHAPTER 6

o you really think Amber will bring the Carpet?" asked Jasmine. The waiting was getting on her nerves.

"The Carpet and the keys would be perfect," said Aladdin. "Let's keep our fingers crossed."

"Are you going to take me with you, too?" asked Omar.

"Much as I'd like to leave you here," said Aladdin, "we need you. You're the only one who can bring Rajah back."

"That's right," said Omar brightly. "I can bring him back as sure as my name is...er...Omar!"

"Oh, boy. I knew it!" said Aladdin. "We're

in deep trouble."

"No, we're not," said Jasmine. She turned to Omar. "Don't forget about the crocodiles."

"How could I forget the crocodiles, Your Highness?" Omar bowed so low his turban fell off.

Just then they heard squeaking outside the door. Then came a click. The door swung open, and Amber was there with the Carpet tucked under her arm.

"Amber! You came back. I was beginning to think we'd never get out of here!" Jasmine said.

"Hurry, but be quiet going up the stairs. The guards are on their break," said Amber. "Nobody around here can do anything without a cup of coffee every so often."

"Perfect!" whispered Jasmine, as Amber led the way.

The Carpet unrolled itself at the top of the stairs. It patted itself all over, shook off the dust, and lay down flat so the group could climb aboard.

It was going to be a crowded flight. There

were Jasmine, Aladdin, and Abu. Then Amber climbed on, and finally Omar. The Carpet sagged when it tried to lift off.

"You can do it!" said Aladdin.

The Magic Carpet straightened itself out and picked up speed. It soared past a bunch of guards sipping coffee. It zipped into the entrance hall and right into fifty armed guards.

The carpet flew up to the ceiling.

"What do we do?" cried Jasmine.

"Go that way!" shouted Amber. "Through that doorway with all the junk around it!"

The Magic Carpet wheeled around and tore off through the doorway. The guards thundered behind them, but there were so many they got stuck in the doorway. The Carpet flew through a narrow arch and down a short flight of steps.

"Where are we?" asked Aladdin, looking up at the tiled walls dripping with sweat from the steam-filled rooms.

"Isn't this neat?" said Amber. "It's the steam room in the royal baths. They'll never find us here."

"Why not?" asked Jasmine.

"The rooms wind on and on," said Amber, "and they look pretty much alike. I've heard that people have hidden themselves in here and never come out."

"Probably melted," muttered Aladdin.

The Magic Carpet swooped through a passage, around a curve, and into another tiled room. It backed out and dodged a large stone fountain.

"Go back!" said Aladdin. "I'm thirsty."

"Me, too," said Omar.

The Carpet stopped while everyone had a drink.

"The Carpet will get us out," said Jasmine. "It isn't called a magic carpet for nothing."

"What are you going to do when we get out?" Jasmine asked Amber.

"Actually, I want to work in the theater," said Amber. Her eyes shone with delight. "I'm a great singer. I dance, too!"

"Really?" said Omar. "I've been looking for a lead singer to be our fourth Date!"

"What luck!" said Amber. "I'm out of the palace not five minutes, and already I've landed a job! I can't believe it!"

"We're not out of the palace yet," said Aladdin. "Back on the Carpet, everybody. You too, Abu. There's no time to lose!"

he Carpet flew off again, zigging and zagging through countless corridors and arches. Dozens of small, tiled rooms with hot and cold running water made up the royal baths. Some had tiny windows, but they were barred.

"Don't fly too low. That water's boiling hot," said Amber.

The Carpet flew higher and squeezed through another arch. They came out in a large room with a vaulted ceiling.

"Oh, my gosh!" said Jasmine, as the Carpet zoomed up to the ceiling. "What's that?"

"It looks like a bunch of statues shooting

flames," said Aladdin.

"There are a dozen of them. They must be twenty feet tall," said Aladdin. The statues had holes in their sides. Every now and then a jet of flame shot out of a hole.

"Flame-shooting statues?" wailed Omar. "You can't be serious."

"What would you call them?" asked Jasmine. "Shish kebabs?"

"Actually, they're water heaters. We're in the boiler room," said Amber. "Tell the Carpet to wait until a flame shoots out of the last one. Then we can fly straight through before the first heater lights up again."

"I knew that," said Aladdin smugly. "I was just testing you."

Abu clutched Aladdin's shirt. The Carpet hovered. Then, when the moment was right, it shot past the water heaters one by one.

"Why do you need all these bathing rooms?" asked Jasmine.

"The palace has a big staff," Amber shrugged, "and my uncle likes everyone to be clean. He's a bit odd. He's an astronomer and needs absolute peace and quiet because he sleeps during the day and watches the stars at night. He's angry because you disturbed him just when Venus was in eclipse. He has to wait another five years to see it again."

"I don't imagine he has many friends," said Jasmine.

"He hates visitors," said Amber. "And music. He heard Omar's group singing in the desert and sent the guards to lock them up."

"I love watching the stars," said Jasmine.

"Well, I think it's dull," said Amber, "and he won't let me sing."

Omar started yelling, "Swords! Holy camel!"

The passage ended in a wall with swords jutting out.

The Carpet veered to the side, just missing the wall of gleaming, sharp blades. But one of its tassels caught a sword tip, which stopped the Carpet abruptly. Omar slid off the front.

Jasmine grabbed him. "Hold onto the edge!" she said.

"Ouch!" The point of another sword

caught Omar's robe and ripped it along his back.

Jasmine finally managed to haul Omar back onto the Carpet.

Aladdin yanked the tassel loose from the sword. "That way, Carpet," he said. "Quickly! There's another arch at the side."

"This is the game room," Amber said.

The Carpet zoomed through the archway and down another passageway.

"This looks safe," said Jasmine.

"No flames," said Omar. "No swords." He began to sing.

"Cut the noise!" said Aladdin. "What's that screeching?"

"It's the walls. Look!" Jasmine said. The tiled walls were creaking, groaning, and sliding together rapidly. The passageway was growing narrower.

"We're going to be flattened into pita bread!" shouted Omar. "We should have stayed in the dungeon!"

"We'll make it!" said Aladdin. "Let go, Abu. Take your hands off my eyes."

"Not to worry," said Amber. "It's easy."

"Now you tell us," said Aladdin.

"Tell the Carpet to fly up to the ceiling. I'll show you a trick."

The Carpet zipped up to the ceiling. Near the top was a small tile with a picture of a star. Amber reached out and pressed the star.

The walls stopped moving.

"Neat trick, huh?" said Amber. "This passage leads to the ladies' baths. My uncle built these safeguards in case any of the men tried to sneak in."

"Are there any more surprises in this bathhouse?" asked Aladdin.

"Just one more," said Amber brightly.

"Oh, no!" cried Jasmine. "More fire!"

"It's a wall of flames!" gasped Omar.

"Genie!" Aladdin howled. "Where are you when we need you?"

"I thought you were going to handle this!" said Jasmine.

"Okay, so maybe I could use a little help," Aladdin said.

The Magic Carpet was so frightened by

the roaring wall of fire that it got an awful case of the hiccups. It started to lose control.

"Say your prayers!" said Jasmine.

"Too late!" said Omar. "We're toast!"

Right then, the Magic Carpet completely lost control. Hiccuping, it flew as fast as it could—right into the wall of flames!

CHAPTER 8

ell, howdy-do! What's shaking, guys and gals?"

The group on the Magic Carpet heard the voice, but they weren't sure what they were hearing. They weren't sure where they were. They weren't even sure they were still alive.

Aladdin was the first to speak. "Genie? Is that you?"

"It's not Harry Houdini, Al," said the Genie. He was wearing a flowered Hawaiian shirt. He had on a straw hat that looked as if mice had been living in it. A banana was stuck behind his ear. "I mean, you called...finally...didn't you?"

"WHERE HAVE YOU BEEN?" howled Aladdin.

"I've been right here, waiting for you — I'm a nervous wreck," said the Genie. "So ix-nay on the attitude, pal. But, hey, you all seem to be A-okay. No pain, no gain, right?"

"Are you kidding? No pain?" yelled Aladdin. "We're stuck in this crazy place with a half-witted magician, a grouchy, star-gazing sheik, swords, fire..."

"So? Presto! You're out," said the Genie. "And you look m-a-h-v-e-l-o-u-s!"

Aladdin wanted to keep on yelling. But then he thought about it. It was true. They were out of the palace, at least. They were still in one piece. The only damage was to Omar's robes. One by one, they stepped off the Carpet.

"You may have a point there, Genie," Aladdin said with a smile. "We did come out of it pretty well. And you look pretty good yourself."

"All dressed up and so many places to go," said the Genie. "I have a hot date in Morocco.

Am I the life of the party, or what!"

"Please don't mention dates to me," said Aladdin.

"Excuse me," said Amber, politely. "I hate to interrupt, but we're not out of here yet."

"That's right," said Aladdin. "How did we get through the wall of flames, anyway?"

"Nothing but colored lights and mirrors," said Amber. "It's a dressing room with a side door to this sundeck."

"Why didn't you say so?" asked Omar.

"Nobody gave me a chance," said Amber. "I was trying to tell you, but there was so much creaking and groaning and hiccuping I couldn't make myself heard."

"Any more surprises?" asked Jasmine.

"Surprises? I missed surprises?" asked the Genie.

"No more surprises," said Amber. "See that big iron gate over there? Open it and we're out."

"What you're saying is that I missed out on all the good stuff," said the Genie. "Why didn't you call sooner, Big A.?"

"I missed you, Genie. But I wanted to see if I could take care of things without your magic," said Aladdin.

"Gee, that makes me feel warm and fuzzy all over." The Genie lifted Aladdin off the ground and gave him a big hug. "You're such a charming prince."

"If you two are finished, I'd like to go home now," said Jasmine.

"Of course," said Aladdin. The Magic Carpet did a loop and landed so everyone could get back on again. They headed back to Agrabah.

Halfway there, Jasmine spotted the Three Dates trudging across the desert. "Look," she called to Omar. "We've found your missing Dates. But what about Rajah?"

"I suppose in all the excitement I forgot," said Omar.

The Carpet slowed down and settled gently on the sand so that Omar and the Dates could be reunited. Then the magician sat down and squeezed his eyes shut. He stretched his arms out and wiggled his fingers.

There was a whoosh and a thump.

"Rajah!" Jasmine exclaimed. "You're back!"

Rajah, looking confused, was sitting on the sand next to her. He licked Jasmine's face and started purring.

"Is that the...er...right tiger, Your Highness?" asked Omar.

"Yes!" said Jasmine. "He is definitely the right tiger!"

"Whew!" said Omar. "Well, thanks for the ride. We'll just be on our way and out of your hair. I hate crocodiles!"

"What about me?" called Amber. "Do I have a job, or not?"

"Definitely!" said Omar. "You can start immediately, if you don't mind walking."

"Wait a minute!" said Aladdin. "What about that other tiger?"

"Don't worry! I sent her back home to India. That's where Rajah was all this time. I sort of got them mixed up."

"Come to the palace for a command performance," said Jasmine, "all of you. But maybe you should practice first!"

"It's a date for the Dates!" said Omar.

"I hate to interrupt, but a guy could feel unwanted listening to this," said the Genie, tapping Aladdin on the shoulder. "I think I've been gone too long. How about if I practice a little magic of my own at the palace? I can be a pretty entertaining guy, you know."

"What about your hot date in Morocco?" Aladdin asked.

"I'll be back before Omar can say, 'Nothing up my sleeve,'" said the Genie. "I'm just going to pop over for a quick dessert — popover, get it? And maybe a round of golf."

A set of golf clubs appeared, and the Genie swung them over his shoulder.

"Better be careful," Aladdin said with a laugh. "I hear Morocco is a real sand trap."

The Genie beamed. "That's my boy! Taught him everything he knows."